Rich Girl, Poor Girl - A Tale of Two Worlds

Asha

Published by Asha, 2025.

RICH GIRL, POOR GIRL - A TALE OF TWO WORLDS

First edition. February 14, 2025.

ISBN: 979-8227826329

Written by Asha.

Chapter 1: A Tale of Two Worlds

Mary had never flown before. As the airport loomed ahead, she could hardly believe she was about to board an airplane. It was the day her life would change forever, and her entire village, her family, and even distant relatives had come to see her off.

They were gathered in front of the airport terminal, a sea of faces full of love and pride. They had traveled for miles by bus, their voices and laughter echoing through the air. Her uncles and cousins were drumming on empty cans and wooden crates, while others sang joyful songs in her native language, their rhythm keeping everyone in a celebratory mood. A chorus of ululations filled the air, high-pitched and clear, as they cheered and shouted words of encouragement in their local dialect. It was a send-off unlike anything Mary had ever imagined ....vibrant, loud, and full of heart.

Mary's mother stood at the front of the group, holding a bundle of twigs, which she flipped over her head in a traditional blessing. The twigs fluttered as they spun in the air, a symbol of good fortune and protection on the long journey ahead. Mary's father, tall and proud despite his worn clothes, held her hands tightly, his eyes filled with emotion.

I'm so proud of you, Mary, her father said in a deep, strong voice, his accent thick, but his words clear. You are making history, my daughter. This is just the beginning.

Mary smiled, wiping away the tears that had begun to well up in her eyes. She had dreamed of this moment for so long, but the reality was overwhelming. She was leaving everything she knew ....the rolling hills, the dusty roads, the familiar faces ....and venturing into a world so different from her own. But this was her chance. The scholarship to Greenfield University...university thousands of miles away, was a gift she never expected, and her family was determined to send her off in the most celebratory way they knew.

The bus was parked nearby, and as Mary turned to board it, the group erupted into one final, joyous burst of song. Her cousins picked up the pace, clapping and chanting as they danced around her. Her grandmother, wrapped in a brightly colored shawl, swayed with them, shaking her beads and smiling with pride.

It's the start of something big, my girl! her grandmother called out in her raspy, yet tender voice. The whole village is behind you!

Mary's heart swelled with love. She looked around at the faces of those who had supported her, their pride tangible in the way they danced and sang. It was a celebration of dreams, of hope, and of the belief that one of their own could make it to the other side of the world, to a place where she could learn, grow, and return one day with the knowledge to change everything.

As she finally made her way to the gate, Mary felt a sense of responsibility settle in her chest. She was carrying the hopes of an entire village, and she was determined not to let them down. With a final glance over her shoulder, she saw her mother's face, filled with both sadness and pride. Mary waved, a small, nervous smile playing on her lips, before stepping into the unknown.

Meanwhile, thousands of miles away, Sophie stood at the airport in a gleaming white dress, carefully applying a thin layer of lip gloss in front of a sleek mirror. She had just finished her second shopping spree this week, having purchased a new handbag ....the latest in an exclusive line of designer accessories. Sophie's life had always been about appearances, and she was more than happy to maintain that image. Her father's contributions to Greenfield University ensured she was treated like royalty wherever she went, from the grandest hotels to the most exclusive Universities. She had spent years perfecting the art of looking effortlessly chic, never allowing the faintest hint of insecurity to show.

Sophie felt a little flutter of nerves, but she quickly dismissed it. After all, this was nothing new. She had been to the best Universities, traveled the world, and met countless important people. What was a little adventure in a new University compared to all of that? Sophie had always been told that her future was secure, that her path was already paved, and nothing could get in the way of that.

And yet, as she watched a woman walk past her, carrying a simple brown paper bag and a nervous glance, Sophie couldn't help but wonder what it would be like to live without all the privilege, without all the luxury. She shook the thought away ....it was irrelevant, after all. Her life was meant to be different.

At that moment, Mary stepped onto the airplane with the quiet hum of the engine beginning to fill her ears. She had just left her home, and in doing so, had left behind a piece of her heart. But she was determined. This was her time.

And so, in two very different parts of the world, Sophie and Mary began their journeys. One was surrounded by the comforts of wealth, and the other by the hopes of an entire village. But they were both stepping into the unknown, where life, dreams, and destiny would intertwine in ways neither could have ever imagined.

Chapter 2: Worlds Collide

Mary stood in the hallway of Greenfield Universities student dormitory, her suitcase in one hand and a small cloth bag in the other, clutching her most precious belongings. She looked up and down the long, gleaming corridor with a mix of awe and confusion. The air felt different here.......colder, cleaner, tinged with a smell she couldn't place. Students bustled around her, laughing and chatting in that casual, confident way that made Mary feel as though she had landed in another galaxy.

A lady in a suit approached her. You must be Mary, she said, smiling politely. I'm Ms. Thomson, the residential coordinator. Welcome to Greenfield University.

Thank you, madam, Mary replied, bowing slightly out of habit, clutching her bag close. Ms. Thomson motioned for Mary to follow, leading her to the room shed be sharing.

Here we are! Ms. Thomson said, opening the door to Room 302. Mary peered inside, taking in the gleaming furniture, two beds, and the large windows that let in a flood of natural light. It looked like a room straight out of a magazine. On one bed, sprawled comfortably, was a girl with sleek, blonde hair, flipping through a glossy magazine.

The girl glanced up as they entered, her brows knitting together in confusion. Um, hello? she said, her voice carrying the sort of high-pitched, polished tone that Mary had only heard in movies. You are in the wrong room, I think.

No, this is your roommate, Sophie, Ms. Thomson explained, nodding encouragingly toward Mary.

Sophie sat up, narrowing her eyes in disbelief. She was accustomed to a certain type of classmate ....well-dressed, well-spoken, and familiar with the world she inhabited. Mary, with her dark, curly hair in a simple braid and her clothes that looked like they had seen better days, was entirely foreign to her.

Oh... right. Well, I didn't realize we were going for the, uh... diversity thing, Sophie mumbled, with a forced smile.

Mary extended a hand awkwardly. I am Mary, she said, her accent heavy but her tone filled with warmth.

Sophie stared at her outstretched hand as though it were an alien artifact, then gave it the briefest shake possible. Sophie, she replied, dropping Mary's hand like it was hot.

An uncomfortable silence hung in the air. Mary busied herself by unpacking her belongings, gently placing a few small trinkets on her bedside table: a beaded bracelet from her mother, a tiny wooden figurine her father had carved, and a worn-out book of poems. Sophie watched with an air of curiosity ....or perhaps disbelief.

So... where are you from? Sophie asked after a few minutes, more out of obligation than genuine interest.

A small village in Kenya, Mary replied, smiling proudly.

Kenya? Sophie repeated, eyes widening slightly. She tried to recall where Kenya was on a map, her mind drifting vaguely to images of elephants and lions. Wow, that's... far.

Yes, it is far, Mary replied with a laugh, missing the slight sarcasm in Sophie's tone. But I am very happy to be here.

Sophie was quiet, observing Mary's excitement with a strange mix of curiosity and judgment. In Sophie's world, people rarely got excited about University; it was just another stepping stone on their well-planned path. For her, Greenfield was simply a place her father had arranged through his connections.

So, what's it like... back in Kenya? Sophie asked, fumbling for conversation.

Mary's face lit up. It is beautiful! There are open fields and mountains, and the sky is so vast. We have markets, animals, and a river where children play. And the people, they are always laughing, singing... very different from here.

Sophie nodded, though her attention drifted to her phone. That sounds... quaint.

As days passed, the initial shock and awkwardness between Sophie and Mary faded, and Sophie found herself oddly drawn to her new roommate. Mary's laughter was infectious, her stories fascinating, and Sophie found herself envying the simplicity and warmth of Mary's world. Sophie had grown up in a world of polished surfaces and cold comforts, where success and image were paramount. Mary's life, though modest, seemed full of things Sophie felt she was missing: joy, family bonds, and a natural sense of belonging.

On the flip side, Mary was equally intrigued by Sophie. To Mary, Sophie's life was a fairy tale of grand parties, designer clothes, and exotic holidays. Sophie's stories of exclusive yacht parties and lavish family dinners sounded like scenes from a movie. Yet, beneath the glamour, Mary sensed a certain emptiness in Sophie's world ....a lack of the community and support she was so accustomed to.

One evening, as they sat together in their room, Sophie glanced over at Mary, who was flipping through her book of poems.

What's that? Sophie asked, genuinely curious.

Oh, it is a book my professor gave me, Mary explained, holding it up. It has poems in my language and English. I read it whenever I miss home.

Sophie shifted uncomfortably. You... miss home? She paused, then added, almost shyly, Don't you want to... move up, make a life here? You know, be more... modern?

Mary laughed. Yes, I want a good life. But I also want to remember where I come from. My home is part of me. I wouldn't be here if not for my family and village.

Something about Mary's words struck Sophie. She was often so focused on moving up and getting ahead that she rarely thought about her roots. Her parents were busy, and connections were more important than community in her world.

After a while, Sophie picked up the poetry book and thumbed through it, scanning the unfamiliar verses. She looked up and met Mary's eyes. Do you... think you could teach me some of your language?

Mary's face broke into a delighted grin. Of course! she said, her eyes twinkling. I will teach our national language which is Kiswahili. First the greetings.

For the next hour, Sophie stumbled over the unfamiliar sounds, and Mary patiently coached her through each syllable, both of them giggling uncontrollably as Sophie mangled the words. As the laughter echoed through their shared room, the walls that had once divided them began to crumble. They realized that despite their differences, they each held something the other lacked.

By the end of the night, Sophie could barely pronounce one word correctly, but they were both laughing so hard that it hardly mattered. In that laughter, they found the beginnings of a bond.

Chapter 3: Family Expectations

In the cozy, dim light of their shared room, Sophie and Mary lay side by side on their beds, talking softly about their lives back home. The subject of family had come up innocently enough, but as they each peeled back the layers, it became clear that family meant vastly different things to each girl.

Mary went first, her voice warm and full of nostalgia. She spoke of her family's small home, with rooms that always seemed a little too crowded but never too lonely. Her parents worked hard.......her mother making beads necklaces and bangles to sell at the village market, her father working long hours in the fields. Despite the lack of wealth, her family was bound together by love, laughter, and the certainty that, no matter what happened, they would always support one another.

We are seven in our family, Mary explained, her voice filled with pride. I have four younger siblings. They are the reason I am here, you know. My family saved for my pocket money and we did a fund raising for the airfare when the scholarship came which was as a miracle.

Sophie turned on her side, her brows knitting together. But, don't you ever... want something different? A life that's just yours?

Mary considered this. I do want a different life, yes. But my different life will be their different life too. My family sees me as the one who can help bring change. If I do well here, I can support them, and maybe they won't have to struggle as much. That means I have to work very hard.

Mary's tone was calm, but Sophie could sense the weight beneath her words. The idea of supporting a family at Mary's age seemed overwhelming. In her own world, there was no notion of anyone depending on her like that. Her family didn't need anything from her; they already had everything they wanted. Instead, her parents expected her to uphold the family legacy, a concept that felt both vague and suffocating.

My parents are... let's say they have high expectations, Sophie began cautiously, feeling an unfamiliar prick of vulnerability. They have a family business that's been passed down for generations. They expect me to carry it on. But honestly? Sophie paused, then lowered her voice. I don't know if I want that.

Mary looked at her curiously. Then what do you want?

Sophie opened her mouth to answer but found she didn't really know. She had never had to answer that question before. She spent her life in her parent's shadow, with her future seemingly mapped out from the day she was born. In her family, stepping outside of those expectations wasn't even considered.

The have always just assumed I'd do what they want, Sophie continued, her voice growing firmer as she spoke. It's not that I don't love them, but I just... I feel like I'm meant for something else. But to say that to them, it would be like.......Sophie paused, searching for words. It would be like betraying everything they have built.

Mary nodded, understanding in her own way. Although her family's expectations were different, the feeling of obligation was something they both shared. For Mary, the weight came from knowing that her family's hopes for a better future rested on her shoulders. For Sophie, it was the pressure to maintain a legacy she wasn't even sure she wanted.

Maybe... Mary said thoughtfully, you don't have to follow exactly what they want. You can still love them and find your own way.

Sophie laughed softly. You make it sound easy.

Mary smiled, her eyes twinkling. Easy? No. Nothing is easy. But it's what my mother always tells me: even if the journey is hard, you must keep going because you are not walking it alone.

As the days went on, Sophie became more fascinated by Mary's stories of her family. Mary would tell her about family gatherings where everyone pitched in, where meals were shared, and laughter was the soundtrack to every night. It was a life that seemed worlds apart from the cold, sprawling mansion Sophie called home, where family dinners were held in silence, punctuated only by polite conversation.

Your family sounds so... close, Sophie admitted one evening, as they both prepared for bed. We don't really do that. I mean, we eat dinner together, but it's different.

Don't you talk with your parents about your day? Mary asked, genuinely puzzled.

Not really. Its more... formal. Sophie looked embarrassed, as though admitting a shameful secret. There's always so much pressure. Were expected to be perfect, you know? My parents aren't really interested in... normal stuff, like feelings. They just care about results. They are always talking about making the family name proud.

Mary laughed, a bright, musical sound. Family name? My family name is only known to my family, she said with a shrug. But I know what you mean. They still want us to make them proud, even if no one else is watching.

For the first time, Sophie began to understand the depth of Mary's family ties. It wasn't about money or legacy; it was about love, survival, and the hope that Mary would open doors for her siblings and cousins one day. This realization unsettled her. She had spent years being told that her family was above the rest, yet here was Mary, with her vibrant stories and fierce love, embodying everything Sophie's family seemed to lack.

Maybe my parents could learn a thing or two from your family, Sophie joked, but there was a hint of sadness in her voice. I have never thought of family like... like something you carry with you, no matter where you go.

Mary looked thoughtful. My mother says family is like the roots of a tree. No matter how far you grow, you are always connected. That way, when you bloom, it's not just for yourself. It's for everyone.

Sophie marveled at Mary's wisdom. Her friend was only sixteen, yet her words held a depth that made Sophie feel like she was seeing her own family in a new, unflattering light.

As their friendship grew, Sophie and Mary began to realize that they each had something the other lacked. Sophie admired Mary's resilience, her deep sense of purpose, and the love that surrounded her family like an invisible shield. Mary, on the other hand, was fascinated by Sophie's privileged world and began to wonder if, perhaps, she could find a way to bring a piece of that world back to her own family.

Yet beneath their shared laughter and budding friendship, they both felt the weight of their family's expectations bearing down on them, like two invisible anchors holding them in place. They both understood that, no matter how much they enjoyed their newfound bond, their destinies were being shaped by forces beyond their control.

For now, though, they would put aside those pressures and enjoy each other's company. In their small, shared room, they had found a space where they could be themselves ....where they didn't have to be their parent's daughters, but simply two girls learning to see the world through each other's eyes.

Chapter 4: The Weight of Expectations

As the weeks unfolded at Greenfield University, Mary found herself juggling not only the academic challenges of her new University but also the invisible burden that had traveled with her: the weight of her family's expectations. Back home, her success at Greenfield wasn't just hers.......it belonged to everyone who had sacrificed to see her here. She carried with her the dreams of her parents, her siblings, her neighbors, and the entire community who had chipped in with donations and prayers to see their Mary succeed.

Mary was grateful, yes, but as each day passed, the pressure became harder to ignore. The endless motivation she felt before leaving home began to shift into an uneasy mix of responsibility and uncertainty, and sometimes, it felt almost suffocating.

Every now and then, Sophie would invite Mary to join her for a meal off-campus, something simple by Sophie's standards but overwhelmingly luxurious for Mary. The first time they went out, Mary had hesitated, watching Sophie order without a second thought, her polished accent effortlessly rolling off her tongue as she called for dishes Mary couldn't even pronounce.

Mary, you have to try this! Sophie beamed, handing her a glossy menu. Mary's eyes skimmed the endless list of dishes with ingredients that sounded foreign and even a bit extravagant. She couldn't help but wonder how much her family would sacrifice just for one meal like this.

It all looks... delicious, Mary said, her voice polite but uncertain.

Sophie laughed. Pick anything! It's my treat. She caught the hesitant look in Mary's eyes and waved a dismissive hand. Please, my dad's credit card can handle it.

Mary did her best to join in, her gratitude genuine, but the sense of difference between them felt like a wall that only grew taller each time they ventured out together. It wasn't that she didn't enjoy the outings.......on the contrary, these glimpses into Sophie's world were fascinating. But every bite she took, every luxuriously presented plate that arrived at their table, reminded her of home. It reminded her of the nights her family ate plain rice and vegetables, of the times her mother went without so her younger siblings could have more.

As they finished dessert, Sophie chattered on about her plans for the upcoming break: a weekend trip to a seaside villa, followed by a winter holiday in the Alps. Mary nodded, her smile strained, as she struggled with the realization of how far apart their worlds truly were. For Sophie, such things were merely part of life's rhythm, but for Mary, it felt like looking into a reality that was as foreign as it was unreachable.

Later that night, back in their dorm room, Mary sat by the window, her eyes gazing into the darkness. Sophie had fallen asleep quickly, as usual, but Mary's thoughts kept her awake. The taste of the evenings rich food lingered in her mouth, but so did a lingering sadness. She thought about the dreams her family had pinned to her success. All the sacrifices they had made; the plans they had woven for her future...it felt like a towering expectation she wasn't sure shed ever be able to meet.

What if she couldn't do it? What if, after all this, she went home empty-handed? What about jobs, her country was full of young people with degrees and even masters without jobs. What would she do if she wasn't able to secure a university and later job even after leaving this prestigious University.

Mary's shoulders slumped as she imagined the disappointment on her parents faces. They had so little, and they had placed everything.......every ounce of hope, every sacrifice, every dream.......onto her young shoulders. Sometimes, it felt unfair. She was just one person, after all.

Across the room, Sophie stirred in her sleep, mumbling something unintelligible. Mary looked over at her friend, with her golden hair spread across the pillow and her blankets drawn up around her shoulders. In the dim light, Sophie looked like a figure from another world, resting in blissful ignorance of the struggles that weighed down on Mary every day.

Despite all these doubts, Mary found herself inspired by Sophie's life, too. She admired Sophie's confidence, the way she moved through the world with a certainty that Mary had never known. In her own way, Sophie was as bound by her family's expectations as Mary was, but it felt different.......lighter somehow, wrapped in privilege instead of poverty. Sophie's family expected her to uphold a legacy, to expand a life of wealth and opportunity. But

Mary's family wanted her to escape a cycle, to build something from almost nothing.

There was a raw, undeniable beauty in her family's faith in her, but at times, it felt like a burden that might break her.

One rainy afternoon, as they sat studying together in their room, Mary dared to bring it up.

Do you ever feel like... there's this huge pressure to be something? For your family, I mean? Mary asked, trying to keep her tone light but failing. She fiddled with her pencil, glancing at Sophie from the corner of her eye.

Sophie chuckled, looking surprised by the question. Of course, she said with a shrug. But it's different, I think. I mean, they expect me to keep things going. Like... preserve the family name, or whatever. My dad jokes about me needing to carry the torch. It's annoying, but it's not that serious.

Mary nodded, chewing her lip. For me, it's like... I have to make it. My whole family is counting on me. If I don't succeed, it's like all their dreams will fall apart. She paused, glancing out the window to hide her face. It's a lot.

Sophie went quiet for a moment, studying her friend. Mary, that's a massive responsibility. I mean, I can't imagine what that must be like.

Mary gave a small, sad smile. It's strange, you know. Sometimes I wish I had the luxury of just... figuring out who I am, like you do. But I don't have that freedom. Not really.

Sophie reached out, touching Mary's hand. You know, I don't always have it figured out either. It's just... different for me, I guess.

As the days passed, Sophie's understanding of Mary deepened. She began to see the subtle weight her friend carried, the way Mary's smile sometimes dimmed when she spoke about home, her family, her dreams. Sophie had always thought her own life was filled with pressure, but seeing Mary's experience cast her own problems in a different light.

Mary, meanwhile, began to understand that while Sophie's life seemed glittering and carefree, it wasn't without its own burdens. But for Mary, the stakes were higher, the consequences graver. Each time she stepped into a classroom, each time she opened a textbook, she knew she was carrying not just her own dreams, but the dreams of her family, her village, her entire world back home.

As their friendship grew, so did Mary's desire to find her way, to somehow bridge the gap between where she came from and where she wanted to go. And though she sometimes felt the sadness of living in a world that wasn't truly hers, she also felt a fierce determination to change her circumstances. She didn't know how she would do it, but looking at Sophie and the life she led, Mary began to dream, quietly, of a life that was bigger than anything shed ever imagined. Themes: Expectations, stress, self-worth.

Chapter 5: The Power of Privilege

Sophie was no stranger to privilege. Raised in the lap of luxury, with her father's connections spanning the highest tiers of society, she had learned early on that her family's wealth often meant doors opened effortlessly. At Greenfield University, her father's reputation alone was a passkey to smooth her way through countless situations that might otherwise be challenging. While Mary often burned the midnight oil, studying feverishly and absorbing every lesson with a fierce intensity, Sophie found that her struggles were different and sometimes, she felt, far less significant.

One crisp autumn morning, Sophie and Mary walked across campus together, headed to a class presentation. Mary had meticulously prepared, going over her notes for hours the night before, while Sophie, having skimmed through the material at best, figured she could charm her way through the discussion. As they reached the lecture hall, Mary's nerves were evident.......she clutched her notebook tightly, her hands shaking slightly as they found their seats.

When it was Sophie's turn to present, she breezed to the front of the class with the confidence of someone who had never been told no in her life. She presented with ease, tossing in a few well-chosen phrases her father often used, eliciting nods of approval from her classmates and even the professor. To her, it was effortless, almost a game. And yet, as she walked back to her seat, she caught Mary's eyes and saw something there.......admiration, but also a hint of sadness.

When it was Sophie's turn to present, she breezed to the front of the class with the confidence of someone who had never been told no in her life. She presented with ease, tossing in a few well-chosen phrases her father often used, eliciting nods of approval from her classmates and even the professor. To her, it was effortless, almost a game. And yet, as she walked back to her seat, she caught Mary's eyes and saw something there.......admiration, but also a hint of sadness.

In the moments following Mary's presentation, Sophie felt a pang of something unfamiliar: guilt. Mary's passion, her carefully crafted words, the way her voice wavered but never faltered.......it was clear she had put her heart into her work. And yet, Sophie's charisma and confidence, rather than Mary's preparation, were the qualities praised in the follow-up feedback. It felt oddly hollow.

Back in their room later that evening, Sophie felt an urge to address the strange sense of discontent brewing inside her. She found herself staring at Mary, who was still hunched over her desk, pouring over textbooks and notes, every muscle in her frame radiating determination. Sophie felt an overwhelming urge to break the silence.

Mary, she began, her voice softer than usual, do you ever feel... like all this, all this hard work, might be... exhausting?

Mary looked up, surprised by the question. Yes, she admitted, a small smile on her lips. But it's worth it. Every late night, every page, every lecture.......this is my chance. My family... they are counting on me.

Sophie let the words sink in, feeling the weight of them. Mary's purpose was something she couldn't quite grasp; her own motivations felt thin and almost inconsequential in comparison. She had been taught that her family name was her purpose, that her life would continue to be a series of well-laid paths leading to a predetermined future of comfort and success. But it left her feeling empty, disconnected from any real meaning or challenge.

Must be nice, she said, trying to keep her tone light. To have a reason like that. Something bigger than yourself.

Mary laughed quietly. Sophie, I think you would get tired of it quickly. It's exhausting to always feel like you are one step away from letting everyone down.

Sophie thought about this over the next few days. She watched the way Mary navigated life, how she approached every assignment with a seriousness Sophie rarely saw from anyone else at Greenfield. She saw, too, how Mary often turned down outings and social gatherings, saving her money, sometimes foregoing even the smallest luxuries to ensure her meager scholarship funds would last through the term.

Meanwhile, Sophie's life continued to feel effortless. When a minor issue came up with her coursework, she was able to set up a private meeting with the professors, secured easily through her father's influence. When she felt like escaping campus for the weekend, her family's driver was a call away, ready to whisk her to her choice of shopping centers or spa retreats.

Yet, increasingly, these privileges didn't bring the joy they once did. Instead, they began to feel like barriers between her and the world Mary inhabited.......a world Sophie was beginning to realize she could never fully understand, no matter how much she valued Mary's friendship. She was reminded of the words Mary had once spoken: You can't understand something you haven't lived.

One weekend, when Sophie invited Mary to join her for a shopping trip, she was struck by Mary's hesitation.

Come on, Mary! Sophie coaxed, trying to hide her frustration. Till be fun. My treat, of course.

Mary shook her head, an apologetic smile on her face. Thank you, but I can't, Sophie. I need to save what I have, and honestly... It feels strange to spend money that way. My family... they would never understand.

This was yet another stark difference between them, one that felt like a chasm Sophie could neither bridge nor comprehend. For Mary, every dollar was a sacrifice, a step toward lifting her family out of poverty. For Sophie, money was simply there, woven into her life as naturally as the air she breathed. And though she didn't say it, Sophie began to feel ashamed of the abundance she had never questioned.

In the quiet of their shared room, Sophie lay awake one night, the words of her father echoing in her mind. Our wealth is your legacy, Sophie. It's your responsibility to carry it forward. She had never questioned it before, but now, for the first time, she wondered: did she really want that legacy? Did it even belong to her? Or was it just something shed inherited by chance, something that defined her but didn't fulfill her?

Sophie glanced over at Mary, asleep in her bed, her face peaceful despite the weight she carried. In that moment, Sophie felt the stark emptiness of her privilege. All her life, she had wanted for nothing, had rarely faced a real obstacle. And yet, Mary's life, so different, so challenging, seemed to possess a depth and meaning that Sophie's own lacked.

Maybe, Sophie thought to herself, I need to find my own purpose.

She didn't know what that meant yet, or how to go about it. But as she lay there, the first seed of change was planted in her mind.

Chapter 6: Finding Common Ground

The first rays of early spring filtered through the large windows in their shared room, casting a soft light over the stacks of books, scattered clothes, and the two young women who occupied the space. Sophie, perched on her bed with a stack of glossy magazines at her side, observed Mary's usual morning routine. Mary had already been awake for an hour, buried in a textbook, occasionally pausing to scribble a note. Her concentration was fierce, her dedication unshakeable, and Sophie was beginning to understand the depth of that focus.

In those quiet moments, an unspoken bond was forming. As days turned to weeks, Sophie and Mary found themselves increasingly drawn into each other's worlds, allowing each other glimpses of their lives beyond the walls of Greenfield University. In doing so, they began to chip away at the misconceptions they had initially held.

One chilly Saturday afternoon, they strolled through the nearby town, stopping at a quaint little café for tea. It was one of Sophie's favorite spots, with vintage teacups and pastries stacked high on tiered plates. Mary looked around with wide eyes, marveling at the quaint decor and the tiny sugar cubes that seemed like a luxurious extravagance. She laughed as she took her first sip of tea, a bit too strong and slightly bitter.

Its... interesting, she said, trying to mask her surprise. Sophie couldn't help but laugh at her friend's hesitant expression.

Not a fan of the Earl Grey? Sophie teased, pushing the sugar bowl toward her. Mary shrugged, laughing.

It's very... sophisticated, we have to sieve our tea back home, Mary replied, trying to be polite but wrinkling her nose slightly.

Try adding a cube, Sophie suggested, enjoying this small exchange as much as she would have with any lifelong friend. Watching Mary's reaction to the small pleasures she had always taken for granted was both endearing and enlightening.

Over time, these outings became little adventures where both women found themselves challenged in new ways. For Mary, each café visit, bookstore stop, or walk through the lush, landscaped gardens near the University campus was a foray into a world shed only seen in movies. And for Sophie, learning about Mary's life and experiences brought her face-to-face with a resilience she hadn't previously understood.

Back in their dorm room one evening, Sophie was bent over a workbook, grumbling over her math homework. Numbers had never been her strength, and no amount of tutoring had managed to change that.

Mary, noticing Sophie's frustration, moved over to her side of the room with her characteristic patience. Want some help? she offered, settling down next to Sophie.

Yes, please! Sophie sighed dramatically, sliding her notebook over. As Mary explained the equations, Sophie listened intently, watching her friend's hands move deftly across the page. For all her polished upbringing, Sophie was beginning to realize how much she could learn from Mary.

How do you do it? Sophie asked suddenly. You seem to just... know all this.

Mary paused, caught off guard. Well, she began, smiling shyly, when you know you don't have any other choice, you find a way.

Sophie took in Mary's answer, marveling at the quiet strength it implied. For the first time, she truly appreciated what it meant to work for something without a safety net to fall back on. It made her own struggles.......passing grades, navigating social events.......seem trivial in comparison.

Their friendship grew through these small exchanges of wisdom, Sophie's privilege and Mary's grit blending to shape new understandings. Sophie, curious to know more about Mary's family, began asking questions, genuinely interested in the people who had raised her friend.

Tell me about your family, Mary, Sophie asked one afternoon, leaning forward with genuine curiosity.

Mary's face lit up as she described her siblings, her mother, her aunts and uncles, and even the neighbors who treated her like family. There was a warmth in her voice, a glow that spoke of deep bonds and a love that transcended financial hardship. She shared stories of her village, the gatherings under the stars, the shared meals, and the songs they would sing together.

I think you would love it there, Mary added, smiling at Sophie. There is a sense of togetherness... of community. Everyone looks out for each other. Its simple, but its real.

For Sophie, this was as foreign as it was fascinating. Her life had been filled with grand events, connections, and the occasional luxurious getaway, but the idea of a community where everyone genuinely cared for each other was new to her. She had always been surrounded by people, yet sometimes felt lonelier than she ever wanted to admit.

Mary, on the other hand, marveled at Sophie's tales of trips to exotic destinations, her family's lavish parties, and the ease with which she seemed to move through life. Though she had initially felt a touch of envy, Mary now saw beyond the surface and understood that wealth didn't equate to happiness or even contentment.

One evening, Sophie proposed an idea.

Mary, let's try doing something simple this weekend. I mean, really simple. Like... I don't know, cook together or something, Sophie suggested, a little embarrassed at how foreign the idea sounded coming from her own mouth.

Mary's face brightened. You are serious?

Sophie nodded. I want to know what it's like. The real stuff. Not just the fancy dinners and outings.

The following weekend, they spent the day in the dorms communal kitchen. Mary taught Sophie how to make a simple dish from her childhood.......one her mother had taught her.

Sophie fumbled with the ingredients at first, spilling more than she poured and complaining about the heat of the stove. But she laughed as she worked, finding joy in the simplicity of it all. For the first time in a long while, Sophie felt like she was genuinely learning something that mattered.

After they finished cooking, they shared the meal together, sitting on the floor of their room with mismatched plates and a sense of camaraderie they hadn't experienced before. Sophie found herself savoring every bite, relishing in the flavors and textures, and appreciating the work that had gone into creating it. It was, in its own small way, one of the most fulfilling meals shed ever had.

Mary, she said softly, glancing at her friend, I think I'm beginning to understand.

Mary looked at her, eyes crinkling with a warm smile. That's the thing about life, Sophie. It's about finding joy in the little things, even when they are not what you expect.

As the months passed, Sophie and Mary grew closer, navigating their differences with humor and genuine curiosity. Each time they shared their worlds, they bridged a divide that had once seemed insurmountable. Sophie was learning resilience, humility, and the richness of simplicity, while Mary was beginning to see that hard work could, indeed, open doors.

Their friendship became a refuge, a place where wealth and poverty, privilege and hardship, faded into the background, leaving only two young women discovering the power of empathy and understanding. In each other, they had found not just a friend, but a reflection of what they both aspired to be.......better, stronger, and, most importantly, open to a world that was richer than either had imagined.

Chapter 7: Love and Lectures

Greenfield University, with its grand halls and sweeping gardens, was full of young love in the air. Students strolled in pairs around the lake, shared secretive glances during lectures, and passed each other notes under the cafeteria tables. Yet, as Sophie and Mary were beginning to learn, love was far from a simple fairy tale. For both girls, relationships came tangled with invisible threads of expectation, lectures, and cultural differences that made the idea of romance as complicated as it was thrilling.

Over time, Sophie's friendship with Mary had subtly shifted her outlook on life, opening her eyes to perspectives shed never considered. Spending time with Mary.......who was so practical, resilient, and genuine.......made Sophie more aware of the privilege that had always surrounded her. Shed begun to see the world through a broader lens, understanding that there were qualities worth admiring beyond wealth and status.

So when Sophie's interest in James, a bright scholarship student from a modest background, began to grow, it didn't feel as surprising as it might have a year ago. James was a top achiever in their science class, always insightful and humble in a way that captivated Sophie. His quick wit and casual charm made him feel different from the polished boys in her usual social circle, and he had a way of making her laugh that felt refreshingly unpretentious.

His world was different from hers, but that contrast felt less like an obstacle and more like a window to something real. Sophie found herself drawn to him more with each passing day, not despite his modest background but perhaps even because of it.

One afternoon, as they sat on a park bench after class, James handed her a book he thought she might enjoy. Sophie accepted it with a shy smile, feeling a nervous flutter that was both exciting and unsettling. Despite her own excitement, she knew the potential storm that would ensue if her parents found out she was seeing someone who wasn't one of them.

Her family had always been particular about the kind of people she was expected to associate with, especially when it came to romance. Her mother had already mentioned, half-jokingly, that Sophie should be open to dating someone from the right family.......one with a name and background that matched her own. Her father's position as a major donor to the university and his social connections in elite circles made any deviation from this unspoken rule feel like an act of rebellion.

One evening, as Sophie and James walked along the lake discussing their plans for the holidays, James mentioned a trip he was planning for summer, where he hoped to gain experience in environmental conservation work.

That sounds amazing, Sophie replied, genuinely interested. I... I'd love to come with you.

James smiled, though she could tell there was hesitation in his eyes. I'd love that too, Sophie, he said quietly. But... would your family be okay with that?

Sophie felt a pang of anxiety. She knew her parents would frown upon it, seeing James as a distraction from her life's path.......a path they had carefully constructed for her since she was young.

Oh, they will be fine, she said, brushing it off, though she wasn't convinced herself. The reality was, she couldn't be certain how her family would react, and that weighed heavily on her heart. Would they see James for who he was or simply judge him for where he came from?

For Mary, her budding feelings for Alex, a fellow student who was both kind and thoughtful, were a source of joy mixed with apprehension. Alex came from a different background.......different country, different race, and, unlike her, he had grown up comfortably. He took her on quiet dates, introduced her to the art galleries he loved, and seemed genuinely interested in learning about her world. Yet each time they laughed together or shared a quiet moment, a small voice in Mary's mind reminded her that there were parts of herself she couldn't share with him.

Back home, relationships were never truly private matters. A potential partner would go through rounds of introductions and approval from family elders, who would weigh in on the person's family background, financial standing, and suitability. Love was, in some ways, a communal decision.

How do you imagine introducing me to your family? Alex asked one evening, as they shared a quiet moment in the university's library.

Mary looked away, feeling a knot form in her stomach. Its... complicated, she replied softly. Where I'm from, relationships are... well, family is very involved. They decide who you are with, in a way.

Her voice trailed off, and Alex reached out, placing a reassuring hand on hers. That sounds really different from my family. I can't imagine that kind of pressure.

It is, she admitted, a touch of sadness in her voice. My family has sacrificed so much just to get me here. They are hoping I will be able to change things for them... financially. I know they want what's best for me, but it's also hard. And they expect me to... find someone that fits their world.

It was painful to think about telling her family about Alex, knowing they might see him as an outsider who didn't understand her struggles. Would he truly understand the depth of what it meant to be poor? Could he grasp the gravity of the pressure she felt to succeed and lift her family out of hardship?

And on the flip side, Mary couldn't shake her own insecurities. Would Alex, despite his kindness, eventually look at her differently if he knew the full extent of her background? A poor girl from rural Kenya? She sometimes wondered if she were being too hopeful.......if a relationship across such stark differences could ever work in the long run.

As Mary and Sophie confided in each other about their relationships, they found comfort in the realization that, despite their vastly different lives, they were each struggling with similar emotions of expectation and identity.

Sophie, Mary said one night, sitting cross-legged on her bed, do you ever feel like everyone already has your life planned out for you?

Sophie let out a small laugh, though it was tinged with sadness. Yes, all the time. Sometimes, it feels like I'm just a piece on a chessboard, you know? Move here, act this way, date that person. It's exhausting.

Mary nodded. I get that. For me, it's about my family needing me to succeed. They have invested so much in me that I don't feel like I have the luxury of... of being unsure.

But isn't it a little freeing, too? Sophie asked. To have family like yours, who care about you so much?

Mary smiled. It is. And I think about them all the time. They are the reason I keep going.

They spent the rest of the evening talking about the complexities of love and family, class and ambition, each realizing that they were drawn to their partners for reasons that transcended wealth or background. Sophie admired Mary's resolve and grounded nature, qualities that, in her sheltered world, she had rarely encountered. And Mary, though unsure of what her relationship might bring, was encouraged by Sophie's openness and bravery in pursuing a path that went against the expectations she was born into.

By the end of the night, both girls felt a little less alone, knowing that even in their vastly different worlds, they shared a common journey of navigating love, family, and the daunting expectations placed upon them. As they drifted off to sleep, they each silently hoped that love, perhaps, could find a way to transcend the barriers between their worlds.

Chapter 8: The Cost of Dreams

Sophie and Mary were beginning to understand the true weight of their aspirations. Both young women shared a common goal: to break free from the constraints of their backgrounds and to chase dreams that were their own. But this journey was not without sacrifices, emotional turmoil, and painful realizations.

For Sophie, her dream of independence and freedom from her family's expectations had always felt within reach. She had the resources, the education, and the confidence to imagine a life on her own terms. But this vision was shaken when she brought James home for a weekend. Sophie's parents, accustomed to a circle of well-bred, affluent acquaintances, treated James with a cool politeness that barely masked their disapproval.

Sophie's mother was the first to pull her aside, her voice laced with barely-concealed disappointment. Sophie, she began, you know we have worked hard to ensure you have a certain... standard of life. Don't you think you deserve someone who aligns more closely with our values?

Sophie's heart sank. She wanted to argue, to defend James, to explain how he made her feel seen in a way few others had. But standing in her family's grand living room, surrounded by portraits of ancestors whose legacies she was supposed to uphold, Sophie felt the weight of generations of expectation pressing down on her. For the first time, she understood that breaking away from her family's vision would mean sacrificing a part of herself.......the part that had always strived to make them proud.

Meanwhile, Mary was grappling with her own challenges. She had left her home with dreams of building a new life, one that would lift her family out of poverty. But the reality of that dream was harsh and unforgiving. At Greenfield university, Mary was exposed to a world of luxury and opportunities she could barely imagine back home. She loved her family deeply, yet she resented the weight of their expectations, knowing they depended on her for a better future.

The resentment sometimes overwhelmed her, a deep-seated anger that bubbled up during moments of frustration. It wasn't that she didn't want to help her family, but the constant reminders of her duty, her role as the one who would make it, sometimes felt like chains holding her back. Adding to her frustration was the unspoken pressure from her culture: a future where her family would dictate her marriage and place in society. Being at Greenfield had opened her eyes to other possibilities.......possibilities that would be lost if she returned home and bowed to tradition.

Mary's internal conflict grew as she became more assimilated to her new environment. Shed started dreaming bigger, thinking about a life where she chose her own partner and decided her own path. But that freedom came at a cost. Each time she envisioned that life, she felt a pang of guilt, knowing that such dreams distanced her from her family's hopes and her cultures expectations.

On one sleepless night, Mary confided in Sophie, sharing her struggles with the heavy burden of obligation. Sometimes I wonder if I'm betraying my family just by being here, Mary said, her voice low. They see me as their ticket out, but... what if I want something else?

Sophie reached out and took her friends hand. You are not betraying them, Mary. Wanting more for yourself doesn't mean you love them any less.

Their words hung in the air, unspoken acknowledgments of the sacrifices they were each making. Sophie realized that Mary's journey was filled with an uphill struggle shed never had to face. And Mary, in turn, saw that privilege did not shield Sophie from the pain of familial expectations.

As the night wore on, they sat in quiet contemplation, both feeling the pull of their dreams and the heavy cost they would have to pay to chase them. They were two girls from worlds that couldn't be more different, yet here they were, bound by the shared weight of ambition and the sacrifices it demanded.

Chapter 9: Summer of Choices

For Mary, the thought of returning home after a year abroad was a mix of excitement and dread. The whole village had celebrated her departure, expecting her to come back with stories of grandeur, wisdom, and promises of a brighter future. But now, stepping back into that tiny village, Mary knew the expectations she carried were no longer ones she could fulfill without feeling a bit like a stranger to her own dreams.

The reunion was nothing short of a festival. Her mother, father, and siblings beamed with pride as they saw her in her new clothes and watched her speak with an accent that seemed unfamiliar yet captivating. Neighbors and friends gathered, ululating and dancing, seeing Mary as the girl who would make it, their beacon of hope. But as she joined them, Mary felt the weight of the secrets shed been carrying.

Days later, in a quiet moment, Mary sat with her mother on a simple wooden bench outside their home. With a trembling voice, she began to speak of Alex, her boyfriend. Her mother listened, both curious and concerned, as Mary shared stories of his kindness, his respect for her dreams, and the way he made her feel truly seen. She confided in her mother that being with Alex had shown her another kind of life.......one filled with freedom, choices, and a world far from the path that had always been planned for her.

But this revelation did not bring the comfort Mary had hoped for. Her mother's eyes, filled with love, also held the disappointment of a woman bound by tradition. She reminded Mary of the sacrifices the family had made, the hopes they had placed in her to return, build a life, and help them climb out of poverty. Mary's heart ached with guilt, torn between the desire to honor her family's dreams and the pull of a different life.

That night, Mary lay in bed, staring at the ceiling, wondering if it was selfish to want a life that would take her farther away from those she loved most. The familiar sounds of her village, once comforting, now seemed distant, like echoes from a life that no longer fully belonged to her.

Meanwhile, Sophie's summer break back in her world felt worlds apart. Her parents, sensing her growing attachment to James, decided it was time to reintroduce her to their social circle. They began arranging dinners, elegant gatherings where she had been presented to young men who carried names of status and power. During one such dinner, her parents introduced her to Charles, the son of an esteemed business associate. He was polite, well-dressed, and everything her family could hope for.

But as she sat across from Charles, Sophie's mind drifted to James.......his easy laughter, his warmth, the way he challenged her to see the world beyond her privilege. The polished manners and refined conversations shed once been raised to admire now felt hollow. For the first time, Sophie felt resentful of the path her family had carved for her, a path where love seemed less important than alliances and where choices were mere illusions.

As the summer days passed, Sophie found herself distancing from her family's plans, feeling the pull of her own aspirations. She no longer cared as much about the family name or the wealth that had once defined her. Instead, she longed for a life that felt authentic, a life where she chose her own love and dreams.

Both girls spent the summer grappling with the weight of expectations.......Mary, feeling torn between the love for her family and the life shed tasted abroad, and Sophie, questioning if the legacy her family prized was truly what she wanted. The summer break, though separated by continents and cultures, became a season of self-discovery for both. They knew that whatever path they chose next would shape not only their futures but the lives of those they loved.

The second time Mary prepared to leave her village for Greenfield University, the excitement had been replaced by a quiet tension. Her family sensed the changes in her, and although shed explained her decision, there was an unspoken disappointment. Gone were the village songs, the branches waving in jubilation, the lively bus procession to the airport that had marked her first departure. This time, Mary had asked them not to gather the entire village; she felt the need for a quiet goodbye. Her family reluctantly agreed, but their somber expressions revealed their unspoken fears.

As she packed her belongings, she thought of Alex and the generosity of his family, who had paid for her ticket back. The kindness meant a lot to her, but it was also a painful reminder of her family's inability to afford such gestures. Shed tried to share the news with them, hoping they would see Alex's family's support as an opportunity to make things easier, but instead, her parents saw it as another sign that Mary was drifting from them and the life they had dreamed for her.

Her mother, who had once proudly packed every gift and trinket for her initial journey, now watched in silence. She tried to smile when Mary reassured her, saying, Mama, I will still be the same Mary. Nothing is changing. But they both knew it wasn't true.

At the airport, the quiet of the farewell weighed heavily on her heart. Unlike last time, when she had walked through the terminal with a sense of pride and anticipation, she now felt torn, as if leaving behind her family meant leaving behind a part of herself. Her siblings stood with their heads low, looking at the ground instead of up at her with admiring eyes. Her mother held her hand a little longer than necessary, and her father's eyes were misty. It was clear that her family felt that Mary had crossed an invisible line, one that was widening the distance between her old life and the new one she was pursuing.

As she boarded the plane, she knew this journey was not just about going back to campus. It was a step into a life that was undeniably different from the one her family had envisioned for her. She wanted to honor their sacrifices, but she couldn't ignore the possibilities that life at Greenfield had opened for her. She could still see her mother's face as she looked back from the boarding gate, a mix of hope, love, and a hint of sadness.

Settling into her seat, Mary looked out the window at the shrinking view of her homeland. She knew she would return one day, but each time felt like a step further from the world her family knew and cherished.

Sophie had always been accustomed to the luxurious way of life that came with being part of her family. The chauffeur-driven cars, the designer shopping sprees, and the constant pampering.......these things were just part of her reality. But this time, things would be different. When the summer break came to a close, Sophie made a quiet decision. She would return to Greenfield University, but not in the same way she had before. No private drivers. No high-end boutiques along the way. She didn't need any of that. What she needed, she realized, was the freedom to make her own choices, however small they seemed.

James, who had been supportive of Sophie's changes, was the first person she reached out to. They agreed to meet at the bus station for the long journey back to school. For Sophie, the thought of riding a bus was almost foreign. She had never stepped foot on one in her life. The idea seemed so far removed from her usual experiences of being chauffeured from place to place. But there was something liberating about it.......something that spoke to the new life she was beginning to embrace.

When Sophie arrived at the bus stop, she found James waiting for her, his relaxed demeanor making her feel even more out of place in her meticulously chosen outfit. Her family would have had an entire team of people to make sure she looked perfect for her departure. Instead, here she was, standing on a sidewalk in the midst of a bustling city, clutching her small suitcase, her hair windblown.

She looked at James and smiled awkwardly, trying to shake off the sudden wave of nerves. I never imagined I'd be doing this, she said, shaking her head as she gazed at the long line of buses.

James grinned, his easygoing nature calming her. It's not so bad, he said. In fact, it's kind of nice. The simplicity of it. You get to see things you would never notice when you are in the back of a car.

Sophie raised an eyebrow. See things like what?

James pointed to a small coffee cart on the corner, where an elderly man was handing a cup of coffee to a woman with a baby in her arms. Little moments, he said, things that make life feel more real. You would be surprised at how much you miss when everything is done for you.

Sophie hesitated. She had spent her entire life surrounded by luxury, and yet, now that she was stepping into the world of everyday people, she felt like an outsider. The very idea of using public transport made her feel exposed, vulnerable, like everyone around her would see how much she didn't belong.

But as the bus arrived and they climbed aboard, something inside Sophie shifted. She sat beside James, and as the bus rumbled to life, she found herself looking out the window at the passing city streets, watching people move about their day, each living their own life, each with their own struggles and dreams.

The freedom she felt was unexpected. There was something thrilling about being in control of her own journey, without the trappings of wealth or the expectations that came with it. She felt lighter, as though the weight of her family's expectations had been temporarily lifted.

James seemed to sense her shift in mood. How does it feel? he asked, his voice gentle.

Sophie turned to look at him, a small smile playing at her lips. Its... liberating. I never realized how much I missed out on, just by being in my bubble.

James nodded, his eyes lighting up. That's the thing about the world outside your bubble.....it's not always as shiny as the one you are used to, but its real. Its messy, unpredictable, but it's also full of life. And there's something to be said for living it on your own terms.

Sophie nodded, feeling a quiet sense of peace settle over her. She had made a decision that had initially seemed crazy.......she had chosen to break free from the luxury that had defined her. And while the bus ride may have seemed like a small thing to most people, for Sophie, it was a big step toward understanding the value of simplicity, connection, and self-reliance.

As the bus rolled on, Sophie looked out the window again, taking in the sights, the sounds, and the sense of freedom that had begun to fill her heart. This was a new chapter in her life, one that she was ready to write on her own terms.

Chapter 10: Rewriting the Narrative

Sophie and Mary had both come a long way from the days when they first met at Greenfield University. Their lives, shaped by vastly different worlds, were now beginning to take turns that neither of them had expected. In this chapter, their personal journeys and dreams take center stage, and for both of them, the choices they made.......guided by love, ambition, and the weight of their backgrounds.......would change everything.

Sophie had always known that she was expected to follow a certain path. Her family's wealth had long been a source of both comfort and pressure. The world of high society, connections, and influence had been the stage upon which her life had played out.......until now.

For years, she had been molded to inherit her family's legacy, to manage their investments, and to hold the social circles they had cultivated close to her heart. But somewhere along the way, Sophie had realized that this path wasn't hers to walk. It wasn't a life that brought her joy, fulfillment, or a sense of purpose. It was a life shaped by someone else's vision.

She had always been passionate about storytelling.......about uncovering the truth behind the glossy images and polished facades that so many people lived behind. Sophie wanted to tell stories that mattered, stories that had the power to change people's minds and challenge societal norms. After months of soul-searching, Sophie made the bold decision to pursue a career in journalism.

When she shared her decision with her parents, the room fell eerily quiet. Her mother, with her perfectly coifed hair and pearls, was the first to speak. Journalism? she said, her voice strained. But darling, that's not a respectable career. Its messy, unpredictable, and... well, it's not what we envisioned for you.

Her father, who had always expected Sophie to continue in his footsteps of philanthropy and influence, tried to reason with her. You have the world at your feet, Sophie. Why would you choose a profession that will only expose you to conflict, pressure, and the harsh realities of the world?

Sophie, though nervous, held her ground. Because that's where I will find meaning. I want to be a voice for the voiceless, to dig deeper than the surface-level stories were told. I want to change things. And I can't do that in a boardroom.

Her parents had never heard their daughter speak with such conviction. Deep down, they knew this was the path she had chosen, and they would have to accept it, even if it was a world away from the one they had envisioned for her.

Sophie enrolled in journalism school, eager to immerse herself in the world of investigative reporting. It wasn't going to be easy. She would face immense pressure from her family, her social circle, and herself, as she tried to break free from the comfort and privilege that had defined her. But for the first time in her life, Sophie felt a sense of freedom.......a freedom that came from embracing her own desires, not the ones thrust upon her.

On the other side of the world, Mary's journey was no less transformative. When she first arrived at Greenfield University, she had come with the hope of changing her family's future. A scholarship had opened the doors to opportunities she never thought possible, but now, nearing graduation, the weight of her family's expectations was heavier than ever.

Mary had always known that her family was depending on her. Her younger siblings were counting on her to succeed and provide for them. She couldn't imagine disappointing them.......couldn't bear the thought of going back to her village without being able to offer a way out for her family. And yet, as much as she loved her family, Mary had always felt suffocated by their dependence on her.

One afternoon, she received an email that would change everything. A prestigious tech company in the city.......one she never dreamed she could be a part of.......had offered her a position as an IT expert. The job came with a handsome salary, an opportunity to work on cutting-edge technology, and the chance to build a career that would not only lift her family out of poverty but also help her own dreams take flight.

But the moment she received the offer, a deep sense of conflict washed over her. This job, this opportunity, was everything she had worked for, and yet, it felt like another chain holding her back. She couldn't shake the feeling that her family would be disappointed, that they would view her success as a betrayal. After all, how could she accept a job that would take her away from them, from her culture, from the life they had always known?

Her parents were overjoyed when they heard the news. You have made it, Mary! her father said with tears in his eyes. We can finally get out of poverty. We can build something better for your siblings.

But for Mary, the reality was far more complicated. She couldn't help but feel like an outsider in her own life. The job, the new opportunities, felt like a world away from her roots, and she wasn't sure she was ready to leave everything behind.

That evening, as she sat in her tiny apartment in the city, her phone buzzed. It was a message from Sophie.

I heard about the job offer. You are going to do amazing things, Mary. Just remember, it's your life. You don't have to live it according to anyone else's rules.

Sophie's words were simple, but they struck a chord with Mary. She realized that she was standing at a crossroads. She could either follow the path that had been laid out for her by her family, or she could choose a new path.......a path that would require sacrifices but would ultimately be her own.

Sophie and Mary's journeys were not without their obstacles. They were both rewriting their narratives, shedding the expectations placed upon them by society, culture, and family. They were choosing their own paths, even if it meant stepping into the unknown.

For Sophie, the world of journalism was a way to break free from the confines of her family's legacy. It wasn't just about finding her passion.......it was about reclaiming her voice and using it to make a difference.

For Mary, the opportunity to work as an IT expert was a chance to break the cycle of poverty, to change her family's future, and to prove to herself that she was more than the limitations of her past.

Both girls had made choices that would shape their futures. And in doing so, they had taken ownership of their lives in a way they had never thought possible. They were no longer bound by the expectations of others. They were rewriting their narratives, and for the first time, they were living their lives on their own terms.

The road ahead would be difficult. There would be sacrifices, challenges, and moments of doubt. But Sophie and Mary had learned that they were strong enough to face them. They were no longer defined by where they came from.......they were defined by where they were going.

Chapter 11: Crossroads of Dreams

Sophie sat on the edge of her bed, her fingers absently scrolling through the photos on her phone. The last few years had been a whirlwind of change.......she had completed her degree in journalism, pursued a career that was true to her passions, and, most recently, had been assigned her first international story. She was going to cover a major political upheaval in a country she had once only read about in the news. It was an exciting opportunity, but it also marked the beginning of a new chapter in her life.......one that she knew would further distance her from the world her family had hoped she would inherit.

She had kept her parents informed every step of the way. They had supported her decision to become a journalist, albeit reluctantly at first. But beneath their praise, Sophie could feel the subtle disappointment. To them, this wasn't a real career. It was a detour from the legacy they had built.......one that would lead her into a life that required financial independence rather than the familial connections and power she was supposed to wield.

Sophie's mother had invited her to dinner a few weeks ago, during one of her rare visits home. Over the meal, her father, dressed in his usual crisp suit, had offered his own brand of encouragement. We are proud of you, Sophie, he had said, his words lined with a tone that betrayed his inner conflict. But remember, your family business will always be here. And there's still a place for you. You can do both, surely? Be successful on your own terms, but also preserve the legacy.

Her mother had joined in, her voice tinged with longing. We have built something for you. We thought... maybe you would come back. Take a more active role in managing things. Your cousins, your uncles...they are waiting for you, darling. Your place is here. In the family.

Sophie, despite her pride in her independence, could feel the weight of their expectations pressing against her chest. Their support of her career in journalism had been given with one hand and withheld with the other, always with the unspoken belief that she would eventually return to the fold.

Now, as she prepared for her trip abroad, Sophie's heart wavered. She knew the path she had chosen would require sacrifices.......time away from her family, missing important gatherings, and facing the possibility that her parents would never truly understand the life she was trying to create. But as the plane ticket to her assignment arrived in her inbox, Sophie took a deep breath and reminded herself that this was her chance to forge her own destiny, even if it meant never fully meeting her parent's expectations.

Meanwhile, Mary's life was undergoing a different kind of transformation. She had embraced the world of technology and IT with a passion, quickly becoming one of the most promising young professionals at her company. The fast-paced, innovative environment fueled her desire to succeed, and she knew she had made the right choice by accepting the job that had once seemed out of reach.

But her personal life, too, had blossomed in a way she had never anticipated. Mary had and Alex irrespective of their different backgrounds was humble and his aspirations were as big as hers. Together, they shared dreams of building a life that was rooted in mutual respect, love, and independence.

When Alex proposed, Mary couldn't believe her luck. The wedding was going to be extravagant, far beyond anything her family had ever been able to afford. It was everything she had once dreamed of: a beautiful ceremony in a grand venue, a dress fit for a princess, and all the trappings of a fairy tale. But despite the overwhelming beauty of the day, a sense of emptiness lingered in Mary's heart.

Her parents had tried to secure visas to attend the wedding, but the paperwork had been delayed, and the chances of them attending were slim. Mary had worked tirelessly to send money back home, supporting them and her younger siblings. She had done everything she could to ensure they were taken care of, but the one thing they wanted most.......to see her married.......was slipping out of reach.

The wedding day arrived, and though everything was perfect, Mary couldn't shake the sadness that weighed her down. She smiled through the ceremony, danced with Alex under the glittering lights, and greeted guests with her usual warmth, but her thoughts kept drifting back to her family. They should have been there. They should have seen this moment.......the culmination of her sacrifices, her hard work, and her dreams. And yet, they were not.

The disappointment Mary felt was not in her wedding or her life with Alex. It was in the realization that no matter how much she did for her family, no matter how many sacrifices she made, they would never fully understand her. She had hoped, with all her heart, that this milestone would bring them together, that they would see her not as a failure for not following their traditional path but as someone who had achieved something on her own. Instead, she had only managed to create a wider divide.

In the weeks that followed, Mary sent more money back home, but each letter and each phone call seemed to carry an undercurrent of dissatisfaction from her parents. No matter how hard she tried to prove that she was fulfilling their hopes for her, they still felt disappointed. It was as though the success of her career could never replace the fulfillment of their traditional expectations.......the ones that had been built over generations and had been so ingrained in her upbringing.

For both Sophie and Mary, the pressure to reconcile their dreams with their family's expectations had never been greater. Sophie's journey abroad was marked by a sense of liberation and uncertainty. She was carving her own path, but she couldn't escape the lingering pull of her family's desires for her to return and take up the mantle. Mary, on the other hand, had achieved what many would consider success, but the joy of her accomplishments was shadowed by the emotional distance between her and her family.

Sophie's phone buzzed as she boarded the plane to cover her first story abroad. It was a message from Mary, one that brought a smile to her face despite the melancholy tone.

I miss home, Mary wrote. I thought I would feel different when I made it, but it turns out the distance feels a little lonelier than I thought.

Sophie typed back quickly, you are not alone, Mary. You are building something incredible. And you have got a partner in Alex who was there by your side. Don't let the rest of it bring you down.

Mary's reply came a few minutes later, a simple heart emoji and the words: I will try. I promise.

As Sophie's plane lifted into the sky, she thought about the sacrifices they both had made. There were no easy answers, no simple fixes to the pressures they faced from their families. But one thing was certain: Sophie and Mary were both rewriting their narratives, and they were doing it on their own terms.

Chapter 12: Bridging the Gap

Sophie and Mary's collaboration in Kenya was not just a merging of their talents; it was also an opportunity for both of them to explore the intersection of their backgrounds and the work they were passionate about. Sophie, now an established journalist, was eager to take on this project as a chance to make a real impact in the world. Her family, though still hopeful that she would eventually take a more prominent role in the family business, supported her involvement, seeing the opportunity as a way to reintroduce her to the broader world of business and international relations.

Mary, on the other hand, had found her niche in IT.......something she never imagined would be her career path when she first left her village. Now, as an expert in the field, she was helping to bridge the digital gap in underprivileged communities. Her role was to provide the necessary technical skills, setting up systems for local schools and community centers, while Sophie used her journalistic eye to document the progress, highlighting the human stories behind the technology.

Despite their different backgrounds, their complementary skills made the project a success. Sophie's ability to connect with people and tell their stories was the perfect counterpart to Mary's hands-on technical expertise. The collaboration was a testament to how diverse perspectives could come together to make real change.

As the days in Kenya passed, Sophie's perspective began to shift. Though she had initially come to document the stories of the underprivileged and shed light on global inequalities, her understanding of the country.......and Mary's world.......deepened in ways she hadn't anticipated. She traveled with Mary to various villages, witnessing firsthand the way technology was beginning to make a difference in education, healthcare, and communication. Yet, it wasn't just the work that had an impact on Sophie; it was the country itself.......the landscape, the people, the culture.

For Sophie, the idea of Kenya had always been clouded by a mix of stereotypes and limited knowledge. But being immersed in its complexities, she began to see a world much richer than she could have imagined. The streets were vibrant with colors, life, and a resilience that Sophie had never experienced in her own world of privilege. She learned to appreciate the importance of community, the emphasis placed on family and collaboration, and the deeply rooted sense of pride the people had for their country.

One day, Sophie found herself sitting in a small café with Mary, sipping on chai, watching the local market bustle with energy. The rich scent of spices filled the air, and the vibrancy of the people reminded her of the simplicity and depth of a life that was often overlooked in the West.

Do you ever wish you could just bring all of this back with you? Sophie asked, gesturing toward the vibrant marketplace outside.

Mary smiled softly. Sometimes, yes. But I have learned that this... this place isn't something you can bring with you. You just have to carry it with you in your heart.

Sophie nodded, realizing that Mary had found a balance.......one foot in her village, where she had roots, and one foot in the world she had carved out for herself. For Mary, the choice to help her community wasn't about abandoning the life she once knew; it was about creating bridges between two worlds.

The deeper Sophie got into her work, the more she started seeing Mary's life in Kenya through a different lens. The villagers who greeted them with warm smiles, the children who ran up to Mary to show off their new computer skills.......all of it painted a picture of a future that was slowly but surely being shaped by the efforts of people like Mary. And Sophie, with her pen and camera, was there to capture it.

But even as she embraced the beauty of Kenya, Sophie began to realize the stark contrast between her life and the life Mary had chosen. Sophie's family, though outwardly supportive of her decision to work in Kenya, saw this as a temporary phase. You are doing good work, Sophie, her father said during a celebratory dinner. But don't forget where you come from. The family needs you. This project... it's just the beginning. We have plans for you, and I'm sure you will want to join in once have had your fill of these... charity projects. His words, though laced with praise, carried the weight of expectation, reminding her that her place.......at least in her family's eyes.......was not with the poor and underprivileged but within the walls of their company.

Sophie, though still feeling the call of a more authentic and fulfilling life, knew her family's expectations would always be there. The business, the legacy, the social standing.......it was part of her identity whether she liked it or not.

Meanwhile, Mary's return to her village in Kenya was bittersweet. Her parents, overjoyed to have her back even if only for a short time, expressed both pride and a quiet sense of loss. They knew that the life Mary had carved out for herself in the West meant she would likely never stay in their small village for long. Yet, in their eyes, she had done something extraordinary.......she had defied the odds, gotten an education, and carved out a career that was already helping her community.

The day Mary arrived was filled with celebration, with neighbors coming to visit, parents beaming with pride, and the whole village welcoming her back with open arms. However, beneath the joy, there was an unspoken tension. Mary's success was not just a victory for her but a symbol of how much had been sacrificed for it. Her family, though supportive, had never fully understood her decision to leave. They had always hoped that her return would bring not just financial security for the family, but that she would eventually find a way to settle down and raise her own family within the village. That was, after all, the life they had envisioned for her.

But as Mary spoke to her mother one evening, after a quiet family dinner, she confessed her misgivings.

Mom, I don't know how to explain it, but I feel like I have changed. The life I left behind here... it feels so different now. I don't know if I can ever come back for good.

Her mother, a woman of few words, sighed softly, as if she had expected this but never wanted to acknowledge it. We are proud of you, Mary. You have done what none of us could. But if you feel like your place is out there, I won't hold you back. Just remember, you will always have a home here, even if you don't come back.

For Mary, those words were both comforting and painful. She knew she had a future in the West, but there was still a part of her that felt tied to her roots, to her family's dreams. Yet she couldn't deny the pull of her new life, her husband back to her new home and country. A life that was far beyond the expectations of her culture, a life where she could decide for herself what path to follow.

As Sophie and Mary parted ways, both were left with heavy hearts, carrying the weight of their different worlds. Sophie, now confident in her career as a journalist, had learned invaluable lessons from her time in Kenya. But the gap between her and her family's expectations had only widened. She knew that despite her success, her parents still wanted her back in the family business. She felt torn between the life she had begun to build for herself and the legacy her family expected her to uphold.

Mary, too, was torn. She was grateful for the opportunities her new life had given her, but at what cost? Her family was proud of her, but they also felt she had left behind the dreams they had for her, the dreams that had shaped her childhood. The wedding to Alex, grand though it was, had felt incomplete without her parents by her side. And while her parents had never voiced their disappointment directly, Mary could feel it in the silence, in the way they looked at her with both pride and longing.

Their paths had diverged, each one carving out a future that was theirs alone. But as they walked away from Kenya, both Sophie and Mary knew that the lives they had chosen.......though filled with promise.......came with sacrifices. They had broken free from the constraints of their upbringings, but in doing so, they had left behind parts of themselves. Whether that would be worth it in the end, only time would tell.

Chapter 13: The Legacy of Friendship

Over the years, Sophie and Mary's friendship became more than just a connection between two people from vastly different backgrounds. It was a bridge between worlds.......a testament to the strength that comes from genuine understanding, respect, and shared purpose. The two women had met at a critical juncture in their lives, when both were striving to make a difference and find their own paths. And through their shared journey, they forged a bond that not only shaped their futures but became a lasting legacy of connection across divides of wealth, culture, and opportunity.

For Sophie, their friendship was transformative. Her experience in Kenya and her deepening relationship with Mary had given her a profound sense of purpose beyond the family business. Returning home, Sophie chose to pursue journalism full-time, focusing on stories that highlighted social inequality, technological advancement in underserved communities, and cross-cultural projects that brought change. Inspired by Mary's courage and resourcefulness, she felt more equipped to stand up for her own beliefs, even when they conflicted with her family's expectations. Her voice became a powerful tool, advocating for people who often went unheard, and her work reached audiences that spanned continents.

But it wasn't just Sophie's career that evolved.......her outlook on life was forever changed. From Mary, she learned to appreciate resilience, the strength of community, and the beauty of simplicity. This friendship allowed Sophie to transcend her comfort zone and engage deeply with lives and cultures far removed from her own. The stories she wrote and the lives she touched were rooted in the lessons shed learned alongside Mary, making her work more authentic, more grounded in empathy.

For Mary, the friendship with Sophie provided invaluable validation and support as she continued her work in Kenya. With Sophie's encouragement, Mary saw the potential for her efforts to have a broader impact, realizing that documenting her work could help bring more attention and resources to the communities she was serving. This inspired her to share updates, stories, and progress reports with donors, organizations, and local officials, illustrating the positive changes Information Technology brought in the villages she frequented with her husband, Alex.

Together, Mary and Alex made regular trips to Kenya, spending time in her home village and the surrounding communities. These visits weren't just about Mary's work; they were about reconnecting with her roots and sharing that part of her life with Alex, who became a steady support for her and an integral part of her mission. The couple often engaged with local schools, met with families, and supported community initiatives, fostering digital literacy and technology access. Over time, Mary's work earned recognition beyond the villages, positioning her as a leader in the field of digital education and accessibility.

With Alex by her side, Mary's work in Kenya became both a professional mission and a deeply personal journey. She was no longer just a visitor from abroad.......she was a bridge connecting her past with her present, using her skills to create lasting impact. Her friendship with Sophie, who continued to amplify Mary's efforts through her journalism, only strengthened her resolve. Together, they created a powerful narrative that showcased the value of giving back, inspiring others across their respective worlds to invest in meaningful, cross-cultural initiatives.

The friendship also gave Mary a sense of belonging and confidence in both worlds she inhabited: her village and her life in the West. She no longer felt torn between them but rather saw herself as a bridge connecting both, much like Sophie had done for her in Kenya. When life's challenges arose, Mary could always rely on Sophie's encouragement, just as Sophie leaned on Mary for perspective and grounding. In each other, they found a sanctuary of acceptance, a place where they could share dreams, frustrations, and triumphs without fear of judgment.

Their friendship also became a source of inspiration for others. Both women spoke often of their work together and the impact their collaboration had on their personal growth. Sophie's articles about Kenya and Mary's achievements shone a light on the value of cross-cultural partnerships, inspiring young people from both their worlds to pursue meaningful relationships across societal divides. In many ways, Sophie and Mary's friendship had planted seeds for a broader movement, fostering interest in initiatives that bridged economic and cultural gaps.

As years passed, their friendship continued to flourish. Their families grew close as well, with Mary's parents grateful for the friendship that had brought their daughter joy and support, and

Sophie's family slowly coming to respect the independent path she had chosen. Both women eventually created scholarships and mentorship programs that focused on providing underprivileged students with access to education in journalism and technology. These initiatives became part of the legacy of their friendship, an enduring impact that would shape generations to come.

Together, Sophie and Mary showed that friendship has the power to transcend barriers and redefine success. They were stronger together, not only because they complemented each other's skills but because they helped each other grow into the best versions of themselves. Through their bond, they created a legacy of understanding, respect, and unity that would last beyond their lifetimes.

Did you love *Rich Girl, Poor Girl - A Tale of Two Worlds*? Then you should read *Roads Full of Idiots*[1] by Asha!

2

Roads Full of Idiots takes readers on a hilarious and chaotic journey through the unpredictable world of Kenyan traffic. With sharp wit and vivid storytelling, this book explores the daily madness on the roads, from matatus weaving through traffic to bodabodas darting between vehicles. Whether it's the absurdity of near-misses, the baffling driving habits, or the quirky characters behind the wheel, this book offers a comical yet relatable look at what it's really like to navigate the streets of Kenya.

---

1. https://books2read.com/u/b5Kg7O
2. https://books2read.com/u/b5Kg7O

www.ingramcontent.com/pod-product-compliance
Lightning Source LLC
LaVergne TN
LVHW090127160826
845673LV00015B/1043

* 9 7 9 8 2 2 7 8 2 6 3 2 9 *